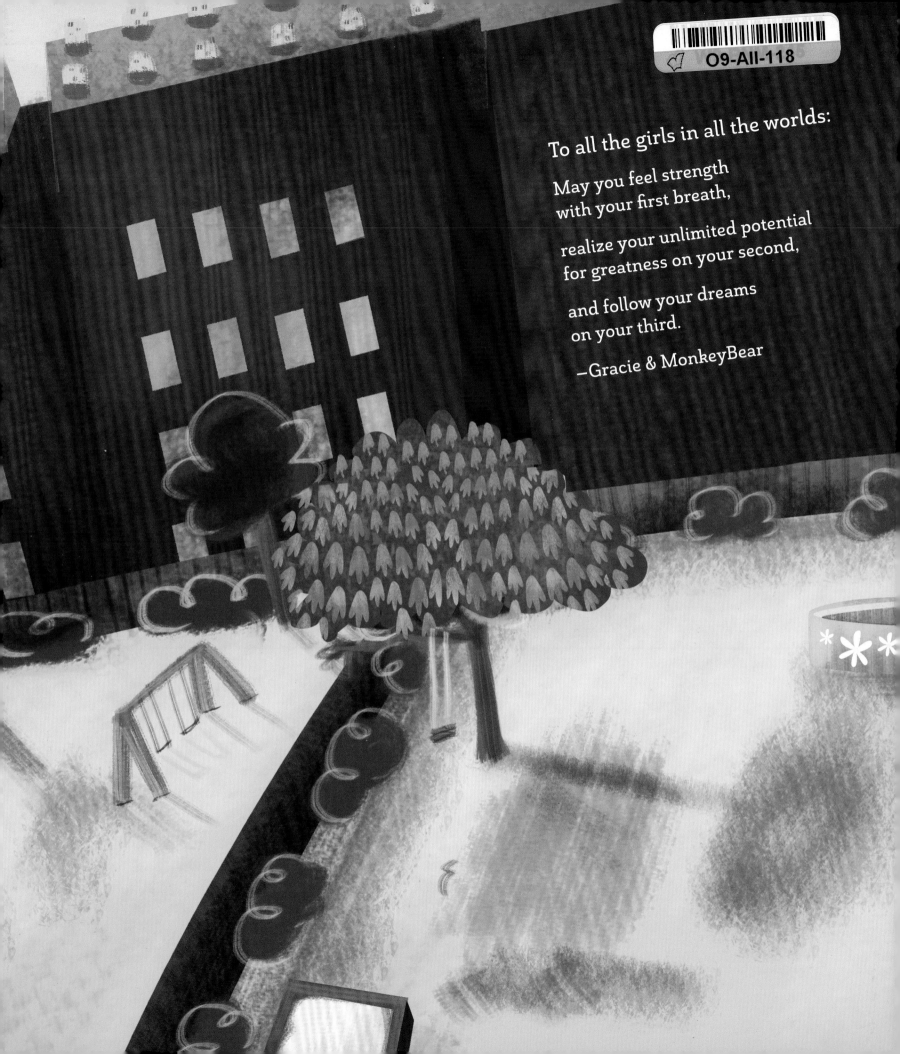

To all the girls in all the worlds:

May you feel strength
with your first breath,

realize your unlimited potential
for greatness on your second,

and follow your dreams
on your third.

—Gracie & MonkeyBear

THE ADVENTURES OF GRACIE & MONKEYBEAR

Book 1: Summer

C. S. O'KELLY

illustrated by JORDY FARRELL

Gracie burst into the room. "Good morning, MonkeyBear. What a perfect day for an adventure. Hmm... any ideas?"

"RRRR... RR... RRRR..." was all his sleepy head could think of.

"I love it!" Gracie said. "What a perfect plan!"

"ROOF?" said MonkeyBear, still trying to wake up.

"Look. Over there." Gracie spotted something by the fig tree
her grandma planted long before she was born.

MonkeyBear yawned and looked for a soft place to take a nap.

"For all the girls in all the worlds!" Gracie shouted.

And like every Saturday before, just as the sun touched her backyard,
Gracie and MonkeyBear were off on their latest adventure.

"What is it, MonkeyBear? Feathers?"

He searched, puffing and snorting, scratching and pawing,
nose to the ground until he stopped. "ROOF!"

"Our first excavation!" Gracie said.

And they began to dig.

"A Tyrannosaurus rex, MonkeyBear! He's been stuck for over sixty million years," Gracie said as a tear ran down his face.

"Rarrrr, rarrrr," cried the sad, scared dinosaur.

"Don't be afraid. We are here to help you," said Gracie, gently patting his muzzle.

"ROOF," MonkeyBear agreed.

"Roar, roar," said the happy Tyrannosaurus.

"Nice to meet you, Stuff-A-Mus Rexicus. My name is Sierra Grace Jackson, but Grandma calls me Gracie, and this is Seamus, but he likes to be called MonkeyBear. We will have you out in a flash!"

"ROOF," said MonkeyBear, busy digging with his bike-tractor.

"Rarrrr… rarrrr…" Stuff-A-Mus thought the world looked very scary and wanted to stay in his hole.

"It's OK. You are safe to come out. MonkeyBear and I will show you the way home," said Gracie.

"ROOF" said MonkeyBear, offering his favorite bone.

"MonkeyBear is an expert on the late Cretaceous Period,
when your family ruled the land. He knows the way home."

"Roar, roar!" said an excited Stuff-A-Mus.

"ROOF, ROOF, ROOF... ROOF,"
explained MonkeyBear, pointing to the map.

Gracie pointed to the sky. "A Voosurian starship is in trouble."

"ROOF" said MonkeyBear, looking into the bright sunlight.

"JungJung ShOOchoo shOOvOO bangEEcha OOvonga gEEtach OObo
[I am JungJung Shoochoo. This green giant saved my damaged starship]."

"Gracie cha MonkeyBear vOOshu rashOOna zOOrachOO Earth orbOOchu
[Gracie and MonkeyBear welcome you to planet Earth]," said Gracie.

"ROOF ROOF... ROOF," said MonkeyBear.

"That's right, I almost forgot," said Gracie.

"MonkeyBear cha mashOOchOO tayvOOka clabOOvo dOOka
[MonkeyBear has a Voosurian starship repair book]," Gracie explained.

"ChOO blantOO JungJung. FlOObOO trOOvo OOrbo pOOf pOOf vEEsh [That should do it, JungJung. Everything is ready to go]," said Gracie as she tightened the last piece.

"JungJung VOOsiarian casOOtOO Gracie cha MonkeyBear rashOOna [Gracie and MonkeyBear will always be my friends and welcome on my home world]," said a grateful JungJung.

"ROOF [I added extra snacks to your starship]!"

"Prepare to launch, MonkeyBear."

"ROOF."

"OOcho vOOsh, pOOvo kEEzOO [Have a safe flight, see you soon]."
Gracie smiled and waved goodbye to JungJung as he slipped into his
starship and closed the hatch.

Gracie heard a faraway song, or maybe it was humming, or maybe it was nothing at all... but something was in the pool.

"Did you hear that, MonkeyBear?" She listened and heard the sound again. "They need our help!"

"RRRR?" asked an upside-down MonkeyBear, feeling a little dizzy.

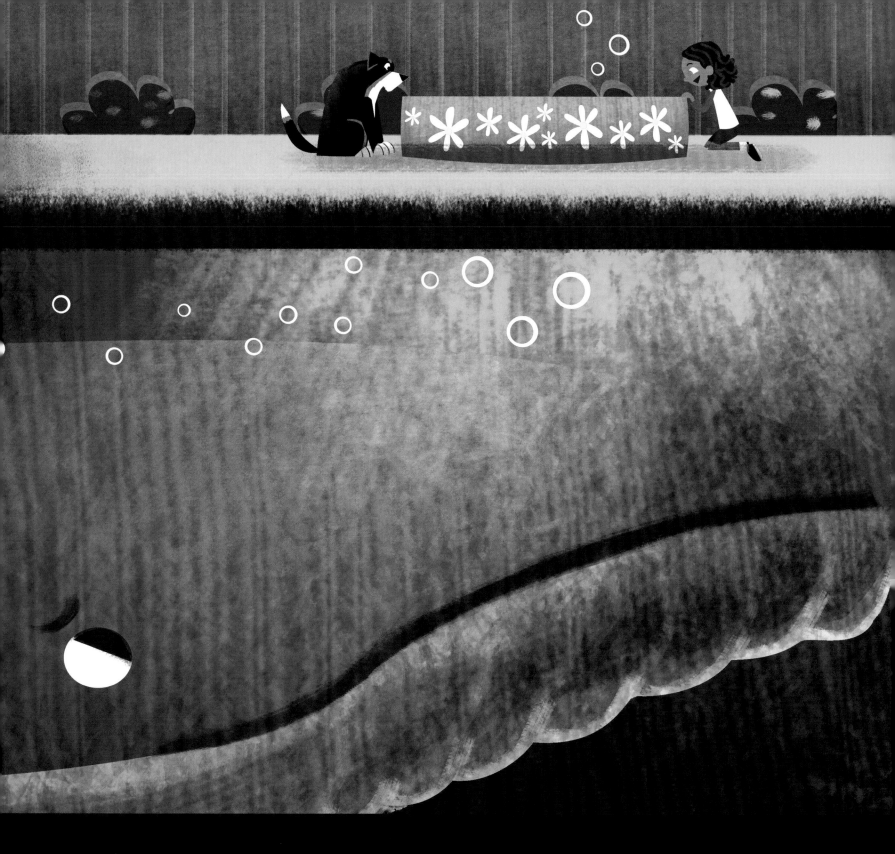

"ROOF... ROOF, ROOF," said MonkeyBear.

"I cannot understand her either, but I know she needs our help.
Can you design an underwater translator and a submarine?" Gracie asked.

"Great design, MonkeyBear. I added a little extra space for snacks and two detachable, deepwater-exploring suits," said Gracie.

"ROOF ROOF... ROOF?" asked MonkeyBear.

"Oh... that is a good question." Gracie looked at the woodpile and began building a launch ramp. "We need to hurry."

"Almost ready, MonkeyBear." Gracie looked at her checklist. "Snacks?"

"ROOF."

"Translator set to whale mode?"

"ROOF."

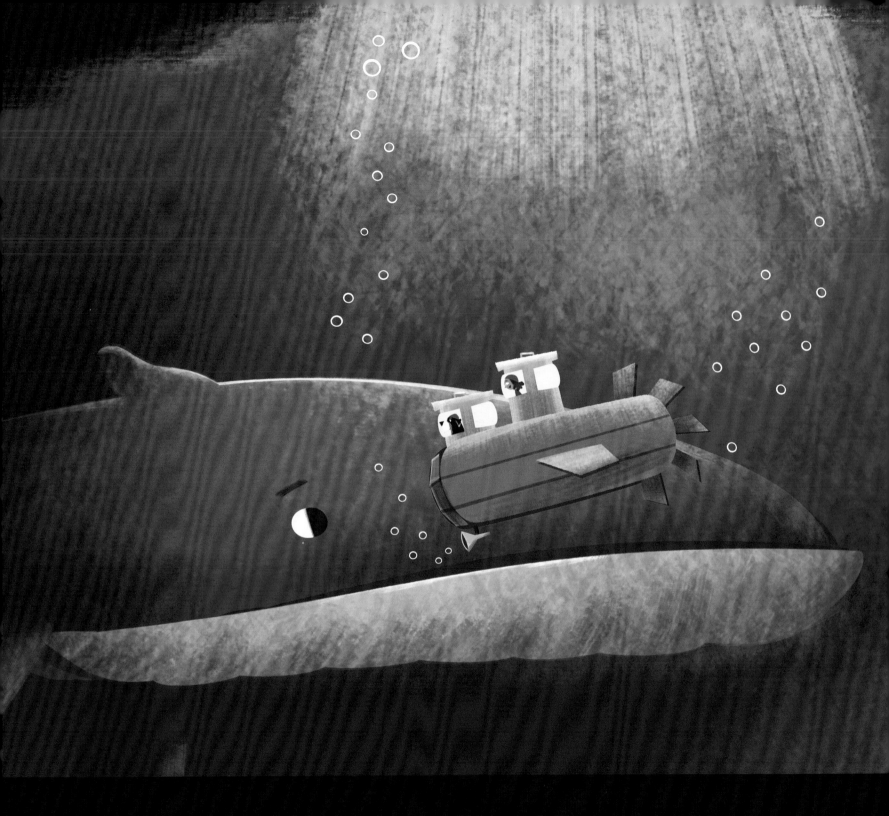

"Wooooo eeee ooooo," sang the mother whale about her calf caught in an old fishing net.

"MonkeyBear, her calf Wooliatha is all alone in the dark and needs our help."

"ROOF, ROOF... ROOF," explained MonkeyBear.

"Great plan. We just need to find lights and something to cut the net with."

MonkeyBear switched the translator to jellyfish and then to crab mode.
Everyone wanted to help rescue Wooliatha.

They just needed a ride.

"Prepare to release the deepwater-exploring suits, MonkeyBear, and switch the translator to whale-jellyfish-crab mode."

"ROOF."

"Everyone knows what to do... Operation Liberty for Wooliatha Wonder Whale begins now," said Gracie.

As they worked to free Wooliatha, far away a familiar voice called out...

"Gracie...

"MonkeyBear..."

...t was time to go.

...Gracie and MonkeyBear waved goodbye to
...all their new friends and floated toward the
...warm light shining through their swimming
...pool, slowly rising closer to the loving voice of
...their grandma.

..."Gracie...

..."MonkeyBear..."

And like every Saturday before, just as the sun disappeared behind their house, Gracie and MonkeyBear were back from their latest adventure and ready for dinner.

for Alexio

Published by MonkeyBear Publishing
An imprint of Lore Mountain Productions
www.loremountain.com

The Adventures of Gracie & MonkeyBear, Gracie & MonkeyBear, and the MonkeyBear name and logo are registered trademarks of Lore Mountain Productions. The publisher is not responsible for websites (or their content) that are not owned by the publisher.

First Edition: April 2016
Library of Congress Control Number: 2016901467
ISBN 978-0-9970294-0-6
Printed in China

Special thanks to illustrator Jordy Farrell, editors Tricia Callahan and Shannon Kelly, and designer Arial Light.
As with all great things, it takes a team to see it through. These incredibly talented and wonderful people enabled the author
to take his story and vision and craft it into The Adventures of Gracie & MonkeyBear. Without them, it would not exist.